The Wedding That Saved a Town

by Yale Strom

illustrated by Jenya Prosmitsky

KAR-BEN
PUBLISHING

This story is dedicated to all the children
who had faith that tomorrow could be better
but were struck down by war before
they ever had the chance to grow old. — Y.S.

To my dear father. — J.P.

Text copyright © 2008 by Yale Strom

Illustrations copyright © 2008 Lerner Publishing Group, Inc.

Kar-Ben Publishing
A division of Lerner Publishing Group, Inc.
241 First Avenue North
Minneapolis, MN 55401 U.S.A.
1-800-4KARBEN

www.karben.com

Library of Congress Cataloging-in-Publication Data

Strom, Yale.
    The wedding that saved a town / by Yale Strom ; illustrated by Jenya Prosmitsky.
        p.   cm.
    Summary: A klezmer band travels to Pinsk to perform at a "black wedding"—an event
staged by the residents to bring a miracle to their town threatened by a cholera
epidemic.
    ISBN 978-0-8225-7376-0 (lib. bdg. : alk. paper)
    [1. Klezmer music—Fiction. 2. Bands (Music)—Fiction. 3. Weddings—Fiction.
4. Miracles—Fiction. 5. Jews—Fiction.] I. Prosmitsky, Jenya, 1974- ill. II. Title.
PZ7.S92163We 2008
[E]—dc22   2007043170

Manufactured in the United States of America
1 2 3 4 5 6 - DP - 13 12 11 10 09 08

"Yiske, wake up! I have a telegram for you,"
said Vevel Valfish, the town crier.

Yiske always slept late after he played at a wedding. Last night, he got to bed just as the sun was rising.

"Yiske, do I have to pour cold water over your head? Wake up!" Vevel insisted.

Yiske jumped out of his bed, put on his glasses, and read the telegram:

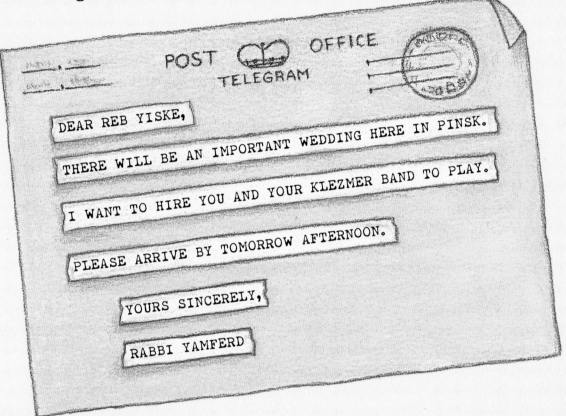

POST OFFICE TELEGRAM

DEAR REB YISKE,

THERE WILL BE AN IMPORTANT WEDDING HERE IN PINSK.

I WANT TO HIRE YOU AND YOUR KLEZMER BAND TO PLAY.

PLEASE ARRIVE BY TOMORROW AFTERNOON.

YOURS SINCERELY,

RABBI YAMFERD

"I love playing at weddings," Yiske said. Then he fell back to sleep.

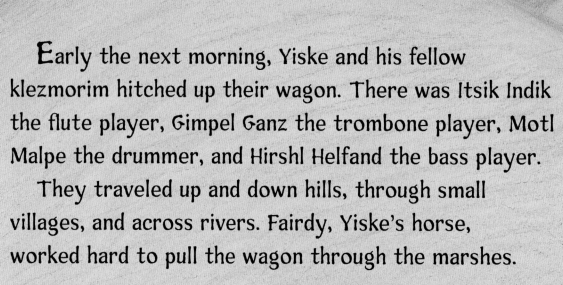

Early the next morning, Yiske and his fellow klezmorim hitched up their wagon. There was Itsik Indik the flute player, Gimpel Ganz the trombone player, Motl Malpe the drummer, and Hirshl Helfand the bass player.

They traveled up and down hills, through small villages, and across rivers. Fairdy, Yiske's horse, worked hard to pull the wagon through the marshes.

Every time the wheels got stuck in the
thick mud, everyone jumped out to help push.
When they arrived in Pinsk, Yiske set off
for Rabbi Yamferd's house to find out more
about the wedding. The town seemed rather
quiet, he thought.

"Come in," the rabbi welcomed Yiske.

"Rabbi" he said, "why is no one out on such a lovely evening?"

Rabbi Yamferd tugged at his beard. "Ay, Reb Yiske, there is a terrible cholera epidemic. The disease is contagious, and people are afraid to go outside. We have tried everything to rid the town of the disease. We cleaned the streets, boiled our drinking water, and recited psalms. There is just one more thing we can try. Legend says that if two orphans get married in a cemetery, a miracle may happen. We call this wedding a *shvartze chaseneh*—a black wedding."

"Why a cemetery?" Reb Yiske asked.

"We hope the spirits of loved ones still live in their children and grandchildren," Rabbi Yamferd explained.

"Who are the bride and groom?" Yiske asked.

Rabbi Yamferd's shoulders sagged and he
pulled his beard once more. "Well, we have a
slight problem. The bride is Sheyndl-Rivke.
But we still need to find a groom."

"Rabbi, the day after tomorrow is the wedding
and you do not have a groom?" Yiske shouted
with disbelief.

"We must have faith that between you and
me, we will find a groom," the rabbi said.

Yiske walked slowly back to the inn. He decided
not to tell the other klezmorim about the wedding in
the cemetery. He didn't want to scare them away.

The next day, the townspeople were busy preparing for the wedding.

Mrs. Yamferd finished sewing Sheyndl-Rivke's wedding gown.

Reb Leyb the butcher prepared the wedding dinner.

Reb Katz the baker and his
wife Sara made the wedding cake.

While his fellow klezmorim slept late,
Yiske decided to go out and try to find a
groom. He went first to Reb Shlomo the
barber. Barbers always know everybody's
business, thought Yiske. Maybe Reb Shlomo
could suggest a groom.

"There's a young man who works in
the mill," suggested Reb Shlomo.
"His name is Fyvush Fish.
His parents died in a fire
when he was a baby.
Oy. Oy. Oy."

Yiske thanked Reb
Shlomo. He hitched
Fairdy to the wagon
and they drove to the mill.

They found Fyvush covered with flour from head to toe. "Excuse me, Reb Fyvush, would you consider marrying the orphan girl Sheyndl-Rivke?" Yiske asked. "Rabbi Yamferd hopes to end the terrible cholera epidemic with a black wedding."

"Is she beautiful?" asked Fyvush. He took out a small mirror from his back pocket and admired himself. "Bring me a picture so I can see what she looks like."

"Fair enough," said Yiske.

"Fairdy, what do you think?" Yiske asked his horse as they rode away. "Would Fyvush Fish make a good groom?"

Fairdy stopped walking, lifted her head high, and let out a loud whinny. Yiske knew exactly what this meant. Absolutely not!

"You're right, Fairdy. Fyvush Fish is too vain. Maybe Reb Shlomo can suggest someone else."

This time the barber was trimming a man's beard.

"Reb Shlomo, I'm sorry to bother you again, but perhaps you might suggest another groom?" Yiske asked.

"Ah, Reb Yiske," the barber answered. "I know just the man—Sruli Tsigel, who works at the carpentry shop. Both his parents drowned in the river when he was little. Oy. Oy. Oy."

So off went Yiske and Fairdy to the carpentry shop.

Yiske found Sruli sawing wood. He was covered in sawdust from head to toe. "Excuse me, Reb Sruli," said Yiske. "Would you consider marrying the orphan girl Sheyndl-Rivke? Rabbi Yamferd hopes to end this terrible cholera epidemic with a black wedding."

"Does she have a large dowry?" Sruli asked. "It wouldn't be proper for me to marry a bride without a large dowry. Go find out if this bride has a dowry."

"Fair enough," said Yiske.

"Fairdy, what do you think?" Yiske asked his horse as they rode away. "Is Sruli Tsigel the right groom?"

Fairdy stopped walking, lifted her head high, and let out a loud whinny. Yiske knew exactly what this meant. Absolutely not!

"You're right, Fairdy," Yiske agreed. "Sruli is too concerned about material things. Maybe Reb Shlomo can suggest someone else."

This time when they arrived at the barber shop, Reb Shlomo was washing a man's hair. There were soapsuds all over the floor.

"Reb Shlomo, I'm sorry to bother you again."

"Ah, Reb Yiske, I know just one more possible groom," he said. "Shmuel Sova works at the well in the middle of the square. He carries water for the townspeople. He lost both his parents in a pogrom long ago. Oy. Oy. Oy.

"He isn't very handsome or rich, but he's honest and hardworking."

So off went Yiske and Fairdy to find Shmuel.

When they arrived at the town square, Shmuel was just returning from a delivery. Two empty buckets hung from a wooden pole he carried across his shoulders. He was covered in sweat from head to toe.

"Excuse me, Reb Shmuel," said Yiske. "Would you consider marrying the orphan girl Sheyndl-Rivke? Rabbi Yamferd hopes to end this terrible cholera epidemic with a black wedding."

"I have known Sheyndl-Rivke for many years but have always been too shy to talk to her," Reb Shmuel said. "She has the biggest heart in the whole village. I would love to marry her!"

Upon hearing those words, Fairdy whinnied loudly two times and kicked her hind legs. Yiske knew they had finally found the perfect groom.

"Wonderful!" Yiske told Reb Shmuel. "Put on your finest suit and meet me here tomorrow at 3 o'clock."

The next day, Yiske and his fellow klezmorim dressed in their best clothes and polished their boots. Then they gathered their instruments and walked to the town square.

A crowd of people surrounded the bride and groom. When Rabbi Yamferd gave the signal, the klezmorim began to play, and everyone headed for the cemetery.

What a sight it was! Rabbi Yamferd danced as he had never danced before. The townspeople clapped and sang.

When they entered the cemetery, Rabbi Yamferd, Shmuel and Sheyndl-Rivke stood underneath the wedding canopy. Everyone else squeezed around. Yiske and his klezmorim played a sad melody. The bride and groom cried as they thought about their parents, who had died when they were very young. Everyone looked hopeful that this special wedding would help bring the miracle they needed.

The wedding blessings were recited, the bride and
groom sipped some wine, and then the groom stepped on
the glass. "Mazel tov!" everyone shouted. Yiske led his band
in a rousing tune, and everyone danced back to the shul for
the party. The celebration lasted until morning.

Then Yiske and his klezmorim wished the bride and
groom good luck, climbed into their wagon, and fell fast
asleep, leaving Fairdy to lead them safely home.

Two weeks went by. Then, early one morning, Vevel Valfish knocked on Yiske's door.

"Yiske, wake up! I have a telegram for you, from Rabbi Yamferd in Pinsk."

Yiske rubbed the sleep from his eyes and jumped out of bed.

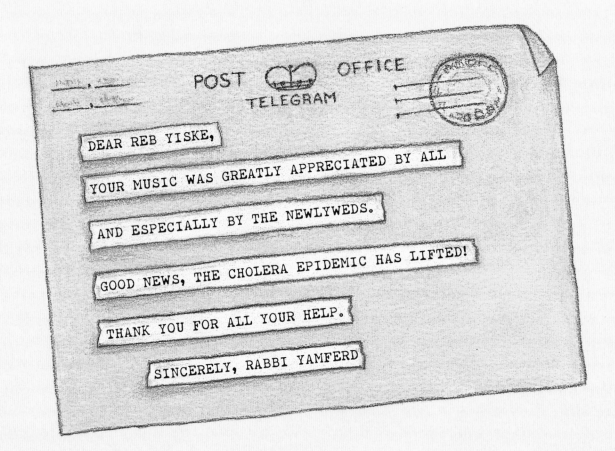

POST OFFICE
TELEGRAM

DEAR REB YISKE,

YOUR MUSIC WAS GREATLY APPRECIATED BY ALL

AND ESPECIALLY BY THE NEWLYWEDS.

GOOD NEWS, THE CHOLERA EPIDEMIC HAS LIFTED!

THANK YOU FOR ALL YOUR HELP.

SINCERELY, RABBI YAMFERD

Yiske lay back down on his bed with a big smile and thought to himself — maybe miracles do happen!

Author's Note

The unusual Jewish custom of the *shvartze chaseneh* or "black wedding" goes back to the *shtetls* (small towns) of Eastern Europe in the days when cholera and other diseases were epidemic in humid summers. When sanitary measures and prayers proved ineffective, the rabbis thought that perhaps a wedding bringing great happiness to lonely people might bring a cure.

Glossary of Yiddish words

Vevel Valfish – Vevel Whale

Rabbi Yamferd – Rabbi Walrus

Itsik Indik – Itsik Turkey

Gimpel Ganz – Gimpel Goose

Motl Malpe – Motl Monkey

Hirshl Helfand – Hirshl Elephant

Reb Katz – Mr. Cat

Reb Leyb – Mr. Lion

Sruli Tsigel – Sruli Goat

Shmuel Sova – Shmuel Owl

Fairdy – horse

klezmer – Jewish musician

shtetl – small Jewish town

shvartze chaseneh – black wedding

Mazel tov – Good luck